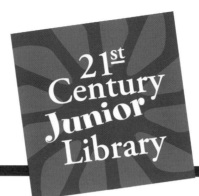
21st Century Junior Library

Exercise!

by Katie Marsico

CHERRY LAKE PUBLISHING * ANN ARBOR, MICHIGAN

Published in the United States of America by Cherry Lake Publishing
Ann Arbor, Michigan
www.cherrylakepublishing.com

Content Adviser: Kevin Allen, NASM - CPT, Metabolic Technician, Life Time Fitness, Novi, MI

Reading Adviser: Marla Conn, ReadAbility, Inc

Photo Credits: © Sergey Novikov, cover; © Rawpixel/Shutterstock Images, 4; © AnikaNes/ Shutterstock Images, 6; © Mat Hayward/Shutterstock Images, 8; © Fotokostic/Shutterstock Images, 10, 20; © Arvind Balaraman/Shutterstock Images, 12; © ivaskes/Shutterstock Images, 14; © Pressmaster/Shutterstock Images, 16; © pio3/Shutterstock Images, 18

LIBRARY OF CONGRESS CATALOGING-IN-PUBLICATION DATA
Marsico, Katie, 1980-
  Exercise! / by Katie Marsico.
      pages cm. – (Your Healthy Body)
  Includes index.
  Audience: Age: 6-10.
  Audience: Grade: K to Grade 3.
  ISBN 978-1-63188-984-4 (hardcover)—ISBN 978-1-63362-023-0 (pbk.)—
ISBN 978-1-63362-101-5 (ebook)—ISBN 978-1-63362-062-9 (pdf)
  1. Exercise for children–Juvenile literature.   I. Title.
  GV443.M315 2015
  613.7'042—dc23   2014021522

Cherry Lake Publishing would like to acknowledge the work of
The Partnership for 21st Century Skills.
Please visit www.p21.org for more information.

Printed in the United States of America
Corporate Graphics

CONTENTS

5 Get Moving!

11 Figuring Out Fitness

17 Active Every Day

22 Glossary

23 Find Out More

24 Index

24 About the Author

A game in the park with friends is a great way to exercise.

Get Moving!

It's Saturday morning, and Nate's bored. He's already watched cartoons. What should he do next?

Nate's teenage sister, Abby, suggests a game of soccer at the park. Abby promises it will be way more fun than flipping

Think! Think about what you did last Saturday morning. Were you active? Did you play any sports? If you got exercise, how did you feel afterward?

Not all exercises need to be team sports.
Try hula-hooping!

channels. Plus, it's a great opportunity to get moving. Abby says everyone needs exercise to stay fit, or healthy.

Exercise is **physical** activity that provides many health **benefits**, including stronger bones and muscles. Exercise improves **coordination** and balance, too. This protects people against injuries. Good coordination and balance are useful skills in sports, too.

People who exercise regularly find it easier to stay at a healthy weight. Too much body fat

Playing with your dog is a fun way to burn off some energy!

often puts a person at risk for health problems. These include **diabetes** and heart disease.

Another benefit of exercise is that it provides an energy boost. People often say it allows them to focus better. Exercise even helps a person relax. It helps the brain produce **chemicals** that reduce stress, or feelings of anxiousness.

Make a Guess!

Why is too much body fat bad for your health? Blocked arteries are the biggest problem! These tubes move blood, which contains **oxygen**. But if fat is blocking the arteries, this makes it harder for the blood to travel. Blocked arteries sometimes lead to serious heart and brain problems.

Running on a track helps you measure how far you've gone. The more you practice, the farther and faster you'll be able to run.

Figuring Out Fitness

What a workout! Nate feels very tired after just 15 minutes on the field. Abby tells him to drink some water and rest for a bit. She says it takes a while to build endurance. This is the ability to exercise for a long period of time.

Nate can develop endurance by doing regular **aerobic** exercise. His heart and lungs will get used to working faster and harder.

Swimming is good exercise because it involves using lots of different muscles.

These **organs** will then become better at delivering oxygen to his body's many **cells**.

Exercising regularly also strengthens muscles. Nate notices how hard Abby kicks the ball. She says exercising every day helps her move with greater force on the field. Exercise improves her **flexibility**, too. She can change position faster and bend her **joints** more easily.

People use different forms of exercise to develop endurance, strength, and flexibility. Biking, skating, swimming, and

An important part of exercise is knowing when to rest. Try yoga as a way to relax.

jogging are popular aerobic activities. Basketball, soccer, and tennis are favorite sports. They all help boost endurance.

Push-ups, stomach crunches, and pull-ups are good strength-building exercises. So are climbing and swinging from the monkey bars at the park! Stretching exercises and gymnastics moves, such as cartwheels, increase flexibility.

Look!

Look at this picture of someone doing yoga. Yoga relaxes your muscles and helps clear your mind. Do you think yoga increases flexibility? Why or why not?

Exercise is sometimes challenging, but it should also be fun. The playground is a great place to stay fit!

Active Every Day

Abby and Nate play for about an hour. Then it's time to head home. Too little exercise isn't good for a person's body. But neither is too much exercise. Most kids should get at least one hour of exercise every day.

Nate wonders if he'll have time for this. After all, he has school, chores, and other activities! He decides to create an exercise schedule to stay on track.

Clearing snow from the ground gets your muscles moving and your heart pumping.

Abby says it makes sense to break it into 15-minute periods. Exercise doesn't just happen on a field or inside a gym. Dancing with friends is an aerobic activity. So is climbing stairs. Helping carry groceries into the house is another way to be active.

Abby reminds Nate that he doesn't have to lie around while watching his favorite TV shows. He could do a few push-ups, stomach crunches, and toe touches. Nate realizes that exercise is an easy and fun way

Organized sports are a fun way to fit regular exercise into your schedule.

to build a healthier body. Now all he has to figure out is how to join the local soccer league!

Create!

Use markers and construction paper to create a fitness calendar! Figure out what activities you have scheduled for the week ahead. Next, brainstorm different ways to fit in 60 minutes of exercise every day. Share your calendar with everyone in your family.

GLOSSARY

aerobic (er-OH-bik) exercise that causes the heart and lungs to work harder and faster

benefits (BEH-nuh-fitz) good or helpful effects

cells (SELZ) the smallest units that make up living things

chemicals (KEM-i-kuhlz) substances produced by special processes that often cause certain physical reactions

coordination (koh-or-duh-NAY-shuhn) the ability to move different body parts together gracefully and easily

diabetes (dye-uh-BEE-teez) a disease that makes it hard to control the level of sugar in a person's blood

flexibility (flek-suh-BIL-uh-tee) the ability to bend

physical (FIZ-i-kuhl) having to do with the body

joints (JOYNTS) points in the body, such as elbows and knees, where two bones meet

organs (OR-guhnz) body parts, such as the lungs and brain, that perform a specific job

oxygen (AHK-si-juhn) a colorless gas found in the air and water

FIND OUT MORE

BOOKS

Bellisario, Gina, and Renée. Kurilla (illustrator). *Move Your Body! My Exercise Tips*. Minneapolis: Millbrook Press, 2014.

Lark, Liz. *Yoga for Kids: The At-Home Class for Young Beginners*. New York: MJF Books, 2014.

Wechsler, Kimberly. *303 Kid-Approved Exercises and Active Games*. Alameda, CA: Hunter House, Inc., 2013.

WEB SITES

Canada's Physical Activity Guide for Children

www.surrey.ca/files /PhysicalActivityGuideForChildren1 .pdf
Download and print this guide to developing endurance, strength, and flexibility.

KidsHealth—Why Exercise Is Cool

kidshealth.org/kid/stay_healthy /fit/work_it_out.html?tracking =K_RelatedArticle
Learn more about how exercise builds a healthy body, and get ideas for different fitness activities.

INDEX

A
aerobic
   exercise, 11,
   15, 19

B
balance, 7
body fat, 7, 9

C
coordination, 7

E
endurance, 11,
   13, 15
energy, 9

exercise
   aerobic, 11,
    15, 19
   benefits, 7,
    9
   how much,
    17–21

F
fitness, 11–16
flexibility, 13,
   15

H
health, 7, 9

J
joints, 13

M
muscles, 7, 12,
   13, 18

P
physical activity,
   5–10

R
relaxation, 9,
   14
running, 10

S
sports, 6, 15,
   20
strength, 13, 15
stretching, 15
swimming, 12

W
weight, 7, 9

Y
yoga, 14, 15

ABOUT THE AUTHOR

Katie Marsico is the author of more than 150 children's books. She lives in a suburb of Chicago, Illinois, with her husband and children.